The story of Walter Tull

Professional Black Footballer and First Black Officer in the British Army

HILARY CLAIRE
Illustrated by Murray Baillon

'Hold my hand tight.' Edward whispered to Walter. Edward, was eleven, two years older than Walter, but he too was trembling. Their stepmother Clara at Walter's side, they stood on the steps of the orphanage, looking up at a tall bearded man waiting to greet them. A large woman stood by him. Their trunk, lovingly packed by their big sister Cissie, stood on the gravelled path behind them.

The tall man nodded. 'Good morning Mrs Tull. I am Dr Stephenson. Boys, welcome to Bonner Street Children's Home. We hope you will be happy. We will be looking after you now.'

Clara hugged them both quickly, and turned away so they wouldn't see the tears flow. They were on their own now. Would they ever see the rest of their family again? The other children had all stayed behind in Folkestone to live with Clara: their big brother William who was 15 and had a proper job, kind, gentle Cissie who was 13, at home today looking after Elsie who was only six and Clara's new baby Miriam.

Would these grave looking people at the orphanage be kind to them? They looked so different from their dark skinned, laughing daddy who had only just died, and their mum.... She'd been dead two years now and even though Clara tried her best to take her place, they still missed her terribly.

Reverend Adcock in Folkestone, had arranged for them to come to the orphanage. Poor Clara.. she hadn't wanted them to go, but she just couldn't manage, not with the new baby as well.

'Good morning Mrs Tull. I am Dr Stephenson. Boys, welcome to Bonner Street Children's Home. We hope you will be happy. We will be looking after you now.'

'Don't worry,' said Dr Stephenson bending down. 'We keep our boys busy and you will learn all sorts of useful things here, to help you in your future lives.' He turned to Walter. 'So, young man, you are Walter I believe? I hear you love football. We have a little team here. They practice in the park.' He gestured vaguely towards Victoria Park which no one could actually see. Walter was not cheered by this news. The park might be green and open, but it wasn't the sea. Not home. Not Folkestone.

The large lady took them to the dormitory where, from now on, they would share their lives with 6 other boys. Walter and Edward had beds next to each other at least, but it did seem so bleak, tidy, cold, compared to their messy, overcrowded bedroom at home.

Now the days passed in school with their teacher Mr Pendelbury, doing reading, writing, arithmetic and Bible studies. The bigger boys also spent time learning a trade in the workshops and the girls learned how to sew and wash and iron, for when they were grown up and working as servants or had families themselves. Every morning the boys and girls had to tidy the dormitories. The matron made sure their beds were made just so. If she wasn't satisfied, they had to do them again. Then, before breakfast, they would have their jobs, sweeping and polishing. All the boys and girls ate meals in a large room. In the evenings one of the staff read Bible stories and on Sundays they went to the Methodist Chapel. At least this was a bit like home, where they had also gone to the Methodist services with their real family.

What Walter liked best was the football. The Orphanage was very keen on the boys playing sports. Dr Stephenson was fond of saying 'A healthy mind in a healthy body'. When war broke out far away in South Africa, Mr Pendlebury showed them where it was on the map, and said 'Many of the young men wanting to enlist have been rejected.' 'Not strong and healthy enough to be soldiers. Exercise well boys, the strength you develop will serve you and our country well!'

What Walter liked best was the football. The Orphanage was very keen on the boys playing sports. Dr Stephenson was fond of saying 'A healthy mind in a healthy body'.

Edward goes to Glasgow

One evening after the boys had been at Bonner Road for nearly three years, Eddie bounced up to Walter, all smiles. He'd been away on a tour with the Orphanage choir, to raise funds. 'Guess what!' he told Walter. 'Dr Stephenson has just spoken to me. A family I met in Glasgow during the tour wants to adopt me!' Then he saw Walter's face. 'Oh Walter,' he said. 'I didn't think. I'm so sorry. But it's for the best. I'm to learn to be a dentist like Mr Warnock – he will be my new Dad. And I will earn lots of money and be able to send for you and .....' Twelve year olds are not supposed to cry, so Walter made himself look brave, even though he didn't feel it. Edward put his arms round him. 'Don't worry Walter. We will be able to see each other from time to time. And it won't be for long. Soon you'll be old enough to leave here too. Perhaps someone will adopt you. Dad and Mum would have wanted us both to be brave and make something of our lives.'

So Edward left and went up north to Scotland. His new family were kind and thoughtful and understood how close Walter and Edward had been. But it wasn't till the summer of 1903, two and half years later, that the brothers saw one another again. The Warnocks sent money for Walter to come on the train to Glasgow. By then Edward was 17, working as a dentist alongside his adoptive father. He wasn't a boy anymore, but a man, though not as tall as 15 year old Walter. They talked about the old days when they had both lived in Folkestone. Walter told Edward all about what had happened to their various friends at the Orphanage – and the ones they'd disliked too! He described what he was learning in the print shop, and told Eddie proudly how well he was doing in the Orphanage Football Team. Little did he imagine, then, that it would be his profession.

Walter told Edward all about what had happened to their various friends at the orphanage.

1908-1909 - Clapton's Catch of the Season

'Here, read this Walter!' His friend Jim, was waving a newspaper at Walter with a huge grin on his face. Only six months ago, they'd been fooling around with a football in Victoria Park when Jim had said 'you should try for Clapton FC, Walter. They're a really good club, and I think you're good enough. Go on, it can't hurt to write and ask for a trial.' The club had taken him on, and within less than 3 months Walter was in the first team! Their team had won every match he'd played in. No wonder the journalist on the Star was writing about 'his clever footwork'. Walter was not bothered to be called 'our dusky friend' in the newspaper. He was used to be being the only black person around after his brother had gone. Eddie and Walter had talked about this and agreed that it was natural for people to notice their colour, but the important thing was that it seemed to make no difference to how people treated them and that no one was ever nasty on account of their colour.

It was true, they'd overheard their father Daniel talking sometimes to their Mum Alice, about being black, and how his parents had been slaves in Barbados, until all the British slaves were set free. Dad had been a boy when the slaves in North America were finally set free too, after a war. Edward and Walter had been too little to understand about this, but they had noticed that Dad always seemed upset when he talked about his ancestors being slaves to white people. They could remember too, that some people had been unkind to Alice about marrying a black man and sometimes people had stared rudely when they were out in the streets with their Mum and Dad. But still, most people were friendly and kind.

Their team had won every match he'd played in. No wonder the journalist on the Star was writing about 'his clever footwork'

A terrible day at Bristol City

It wasn't just the newspaper reporter for the Football Star who'd noticed Walter. He had been spotted by a scout from Tottenham Hotspurs, always on the lookout for new talent. Within a few months Walter had left Clapton and was signed up to play for Spurs 'A' and Reserve teams, and then their first team. Then came some really exciting news. The Spurs First Team was going on tour to South America, and Walter would be going too! Poor Walter was terribly sea sick on the voyage but when the team got back to England, he was selected for Spurs first-ever First Division game. The first few away games in the First Team were not a huge success for Walter, but the home game against Manchester United was a triumph. Walter pinned the newspaper report saying 'Tull is very good indeed' next to his mirror.

But suddenly, things started to go very wrong.

It was a mild October day and Spurs was playing Bristol City away. Away matches are always harder than Home games. The other team has so many more supporters cheering them on and they know their own ground. But something worse was happening. At first Walter thought the crowd was cheering him as he dribbled the ball up the field, then passed it to the centre forward. But then loud and clear he heard what they were shouting. They were screaming horrible words about his colour, calling him names that no one had ever called him before. He felt himself sweating. 'Concentrate on the game, concentrate' he whispered to himself. Don't let them put you off.' Back in the dressing rooms, his mates came up to him. They could see he was upset. 'Take no notice,' someone said. 'They're ignorant hooligans, you're a much better man than any of them. Sticks and stones, Walter, remember, sticks and stones. Don't let them win by getting at you.' The trouble was that words really did hurt, perhaps more than sticks and stones. Walter felt a bit better the next day, after he'd read the report in the newspaper praising him and condemning the ugly racism.

'Tull is so clean in mind and method as to be a model for all white men who play football, whether they be amateur or professional. In point of ability, if not in actual achievement, Tull was the best forward on the field.'

But still he found it hard to forget the memory of those hate-filled people, who didn't even know him, shouting from beyond the pitch.

Tull was the best forward on the field.

Northampton Cobblers

Somehow things were never right again at Spurs, after the dreadful day at Bristol. Some of Walter's mates thought that the managers had been upset by the racism. But instead of supporting Walter, they decided to leave him out of the big matches to avoid further trouble. Walter wasn't sure what to think of this. When he was sent down to the Reserves he wasn't the type to try and find excuses. The long years at the Orphanage had taught him that you have to keep going, even when the going is tough. But when the Cobblers' Manager Herbert Spencer invited him to transfer to Northampton Town, he decided to go. He moved up to Northampton and found lodgings in Rushden, with another member of the team, Eric Tomkins.

They were good years with the Cobblers. He was one of their best players. He played in more than a hundred games, and in one match he scored four goals! The crowds loved him.

Now several teams were trying to buy him. He was most tempted by Rangers, a Premier team in Glasgow, his brother Eddie's home town. How wonderful it would be to live near him again and see him as often as he liked!

They were good years with the Cobblers.
He was one of their best players.

The world is about to change for ever....

1914 was a lovely summer. The news in June that Archduke Franz Ferdinand of Austria-Hungary had been killed didn't really worry Walter and his friends. In the beginning, they thought it was nothing to do with them, a murder far away! But in August the news came that Britain had declared war on Germany. It was partly because Archduke Franz Ferdinand had been killed. Lord Kitchener, who had been in charge in South Africa during the South African War, was asking for 100,000 men to join the British Army.

Lord Kitchener was asking for 100,000 men to join the British Army.

Still, like everyone else, Walter and his friends thought the war would all be over by Christmas. When Christmas came, everyone cheered to hear about the football matches between German and English soldiers. All over the battle front, they had come together in No Man's Land and given each other presents and sung Christmas carols together.

Still, like everyone else, Walter and his friends thought the war would all be over by Christmas. When Christmas came, everyone cheered to hear about the football matches between German and English soldiers. All over the battle front, they had come together in No Man's Land and given each other presents and sung Christmas carols together.

Sent home to recover...

Walter felt terrible. His feet hurt, his head was spinning, he felt as if he was going crazy. The noise of the guns continued to batter his brain, even when all was silent. His dreams and his waking hours were haunted by pictures of his dead and wounded friends. He couldn't concentrate on anything.

Now a doctor was bending over him, reassuring him.

'It's alright Sergeant,' he was saying. 'We're sending you home for a rest. You're suffering from shellshock, and your feet are a mess from living in the mud for so long.'

It took several months to recover but then he was sent back to France for another three months. Back in England again at Christmas time, there was a huge surprise! He'd been to see his family and now he was in Rushden, staying with friends he'd known from his days with the Cobblers. Walter expected instructions to return to France. But instead, a letter came saying he had been recommended for officer training in Scotland. It was such a shock that Walter had to sit down to take in the news. It seems he'd been praised for his leadership qualities and good sense and for being popular with his fellow soldiers. When he went back to the Front after his training, he would be in charge of other men.

Packing up his few belongings ready to go north to Scotland, Walter could hardly contain his excitement. An officer! Him? Little Walter from the Bethnal Green Orphanage? Just wait till he told Eddie!

He knew the rules in the Army as well as anyone. It was written down in black and white. 'No negro or person of colour to occupy officer rank.' Had the army simply decided to ignore the rule? His thoughts turned immediately to his family. Mum and Dad would have been so proud if they could only have known. His brothers and sisters and stepmother Clara would be overjoyed on his behalf, even if they worried about him going back to the Front. Stern Dr Stephenson and his teacher Mr Pendelbury would be delighted about the honour to a Bonner Road boy.

Well, he would show all those who didn't believe black people were as good as white.... For a moment the memory of the dreadful day at Bristol came back into his mind. Then he quickly turned his thoughts to the future.

Walter expected instructions to return to France. But instead, a letter came saying he had been recommended for officer training in Scotland.

Soon Walter was back at the battle. They were in Flanders now, in a place called Passchendaele. There was a little town called Ypres they were supposed to defend, and the soldiers called it Wipers for a joke.

Walter was in a new regiment now, the 23rd, but still with other footballers. Once more they were on the move. This time they were going to Italy, near a river called the Piave. Walter did something very brave. He led his men across the Piave to the other side, and brought them safely back again, without losing a single man. Major General Sir Sydney Lawford, commanding officer, sent back a report about the battle and singled Walter out for a special mention in his Dispatches.

'I wish to place on record' it said, 'my appreciation of your gallantry and coolness. You were one of the first to cross the river prior to the raid, and during the raid you took the covering party of the main body across and brought them back, without a casualty, in spite of heavy fire.'

Walter was mentioned by name for 'gallantry and coolness' under attack.

This time there were going to Italy, near a river called the Piave. Walter was mentioned by name for 'Gallantry and Coolness' under attack.

The last months

After being in Italy, his battalion had a short rest back in England. Then they were transferred back to France, to the terrible Somme Valley. Only a year before, the Somme had been the graveyard of four hundred and twenty thousand British soldiers, even more Germans and two hundred thousand French, all killed in a futile effort to gain a few square metres of land.

163 thousand British soldiers died at the second battle of the Somme. One of them was Second Lieutenant Walter Tull.

Private Billingham was only a few metres away from his friend when Walter staggered and fell. Thomas rushed forward though the machine guns were blasting all round. 'Hold on, Walter,' he cried. 'Hold on, we'll get you back to safety.'

But it was too late. Gentle Walter, everyone's friend was dead. Private Billingham lifted the lifeless body and ran. But the Germans were almost upon them. He gently laid down his friend on the muddy battleground. 'Goodbye Walter, rest in peace. We will miss you,' he said.

Walter's body was never found. He became one of the thousands buried in anonymous graves in the fields of France.

The war ended that same year, on the 11th hour of the 11th day of the 11th month of 1918, the leaders on both sides signed the Armistice agreement, ending the war.

Walter's body was never found. He became one of the thousands buried in anonymous graves in the fields of France.

Northampton honours Walter

It is Sunday, July 11th 1999. Walter died more than 80 years ago, but he has not been forgotten. Today a large crowd of important people has gathered round a huge slab of marble, black and white squares, covered with writing. School children from Northampton listen as the Deputy High Commissioner of Barbados speaks about Walter. They lay wreaths at the foot of the marble.

Walter Tull, the first black professional footballer in Britain, the first black officer in the British Army is, at last, being publicly honoured.

'WDJ Tull ridiculed the barriers of ignorance that tried to deny people of colour equality ... his life stands testament to a determination to confront those people.'

Glossary

Anonymous
Without a name

Commission
Walter's rank in the beginning was a sergeant. This was a Non Commissioned Officer. Officers who were 'commissioned' went through a special training.

Deadlock
A period when nothing seems to change, neither the Germans nor the British army can make any headway.

Dispatches
Reports sent from battles back to headquarters which make special mention of soldiers who have been particularly brave.

Dormitory
A large room with several beds where the boys would all sleep.

The Front
This is the name given to the battle area where the British soldiers fought directly with enemy troops. Quite often, the Front was at a river – like the Somme in Normandy and the Piave in Italy. Walter fought at both these Fronts.

Orphanage
A home for children who have lost their parents, where they will be looked after. These days usually called a 'Children's Home'.